what i must tell the world

HOW LORRAINE HANSBERRY FOUND HER VOICE

To all the children with stories to tell.
The world is listening.
—Jay Leslie

To Bisan Owda—
for your powerful voice, courage,
and for all that you told the world!
—Loveis Wise

HILLMAN GRAD BOOKS
A zando IMPRINT

what i must tell the world

HOW LORRAINE HANSBERRY FOUND HER VOICE

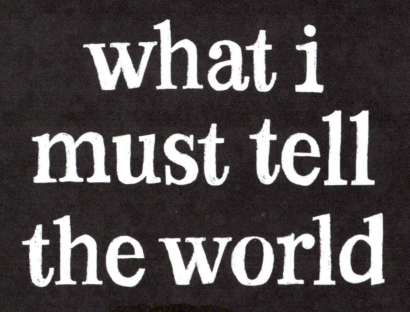

WORDS BY
JAY LESLIE

PICTURES BY
LOVEIS WISE

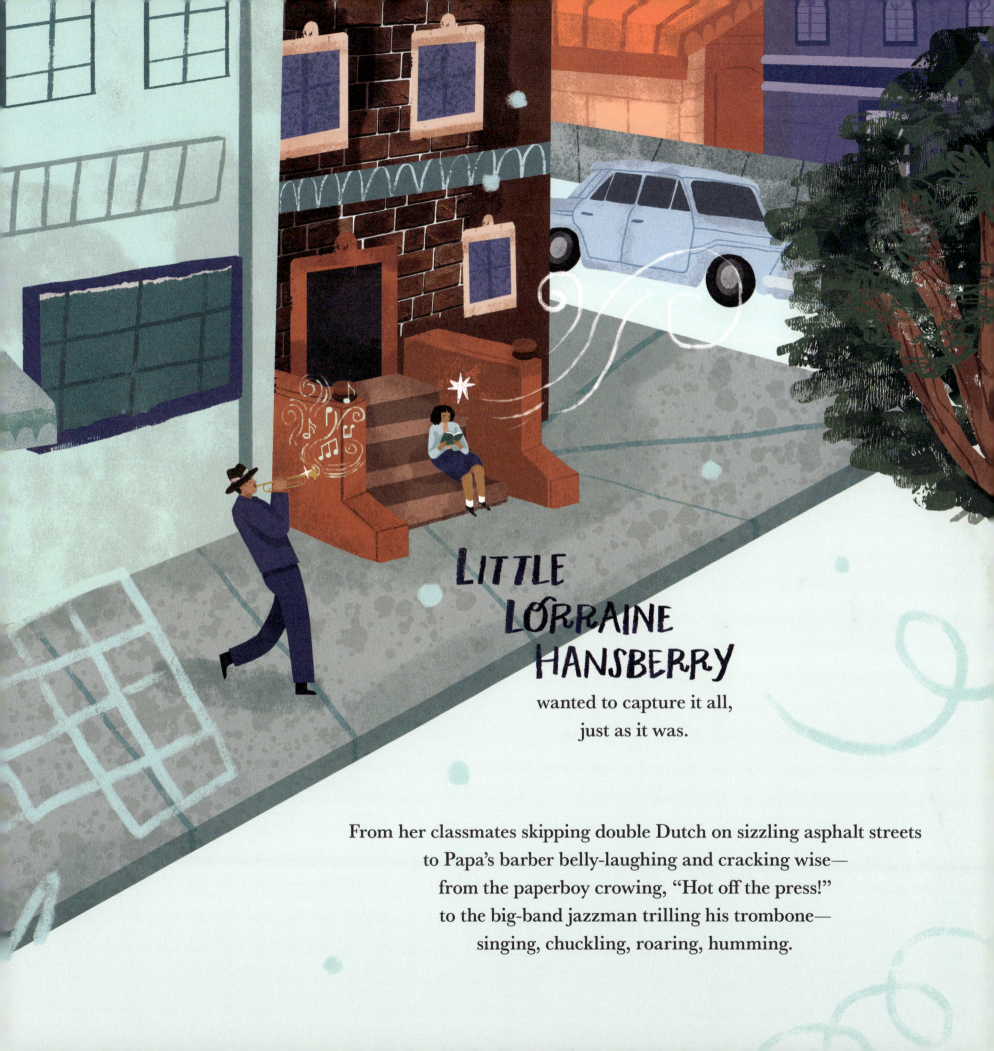

LITTLE LORRAINE HANSBERRY

wanted to capture it all,
just as it was.

From her classmates skipping double Dutch on sizzling asphalt streets
to Papa's barber belly-laughing and cracking wise—
from the paperboy crowing, "Hot off the press!"
to the big-band jazzman trilling his trombone—
singing, chuckling, roaring, humming.

But there was one story she didn't understand:

WHITE TENANTS ONLY

In the 1930s, the city of Chicago was a city sliced in two. As soon as Black folks crossed from Bronzeville into Woodlawn, on the white side, they had to hang their heads and go quiet.

Like all the sounds and stories inside of them had shriveled up and turned to dust.

One night, Lorraine's parents, Carl and Louise, sat the entire family down.

Mama's voice was gentle.
"You know your papa and I always speak up for what's right."

Papa's voice thundered: "It's time to speak up again!
By living where they say people
like us aren't supposed to live.
By showing the world
we belong everywhere."

Mama handed Lorraine a suitcase.
"We're moving to Woodlawn."

"Mama!" She gulped.
"Isn't Woodlawn for white folks?"

"No, Lorraine, Black folks like us belong there
too. Someone has to be the first to say so."

Lorraine bounced with excitement.
They would bring their own sounds, their own stories to Woodlawn.

But the morning Lorraine's family moved in, her new neighbors spat and sneered and shook their heads. Their whispers followed her.

"BLACK PEOPLE LIE AND STEAL."

"THEY DON'T TALK RIGHT."

"THEY DON'T GO TO SCHOOL."

Lorraine wanted to say *We belong here too.*
But the fury in their eyes kept her silent.

One night, Lorraine was playing at home with her older sister. Suddenly:

SMASH!

Outside, a white mob chanted:

"GO BACK TO BRONZEVILLE!"

Lorraine was scared. "Papa, I want to go home."

"No, this *is* home, Lorraine. We bought this house fair and square. They want to push us out. They want to take away our voice—because that's our most powerful weapon. Because even if they hurt our bodies, our words live on forever. OUR STORIES CAN CHANGE THE WORLD."

To prove they had the right to live in Woodlawn, the Hansberrys went to the highest court in the United States. The case was *Hansberry v. Lee*.

At the Supreme Court, Lorraine's parents stood strong.
"White mobs spread lies about Black folks, but here's our truth:
We've worked hard to give our children the world—the *whole* world.
We dream of an America where everyone is equal.
Where everyone is heard!"

They envisioned the world not as it was, but as it *could be*.

The Supreme Court ruled in favor of the Hansberrys.

They Had Won The Case!

After their victory, other Black families moved to Woodlawn, and soon their homes filled with laughter and jazz. Famous African-American thinkers traveled all the way from New York City just to shake her parents' hands. Lorraine dreamed of becoming just like them.

Would she become a mesmerizing musician like DUKE ELLINGTON?

An astonishing artist like PAUL ROBESON?

A powerful poet like **LANGSTON HUGHES?**

Or even an earth-shaking orator like her father?

"THE WORLD LISTENED," Lorraine whispered in awe.

Lorraine tried writing fiction and poetry, but the stories wouldn't come alive.
She wanted to capture the people she saw, just as they were.

The answer came when she was fourteen.
The answer came when she went to see a play.

She was sucked into another world, where she lived a family's pain and struggles,
trials and triumphs, as if they were her own. They didn't use big words—
no, sir, they spoke like regular people. She was reminded of
bustling Bronzeville streets, bursting and booming with life and sound.

Plays didn't show the world as it was—
but as it could be.

A lightbulb went off.

THEATER.

"I can share the **STORIES** of Bronzeville on the stage."

With theater, Lorraine's words could **ECHO** out for all to hear.

Even though Lorraine's family had won their landmark case, Chicago was still split in two. America was still fracturing along the fault lines of race.

"WITH THEATER, I CAN CONTINUE WHAT MAMA AND PAPA STARTED."

Sadly, Lorraine's father never got to see her realize this dream. Papa had always been a fighter, but resisting America's racism had made him tired, and sick, and eventually it took his life.

Lorraine and her family grieved
a life cut
too short.

"Is this the price of speaking up?" she asked herself.

Papa's voice echoed in her heart:
WORDS LIVE ON FOREVER.

Lorraine promised, "Papa's words *will* live on forever, through me. I will speak for him and for those who have been silenced."

For *Freedom*, Lorraine wrote about activists turning America upside down, Black revolutionaries like her parents who fought for:

She joined picket lines and protests and cried out for change—
how could she accept the broken world as it was, when she knew what it could be?

Lorraine was good at writing about other people. Maybe *too* good.
Her work at *Freedom* meant she had little time for her own stories.

Lorraine still dreamed of writing for the stage,
but did anyone really want to hear
what she had to say?

After all,
she wasn't like Robeson
or Du Bois
or even her parents.

She was a young,
unmarried
Black woman.

Lorraine had never thought about marriage before,
but now it sounded like another story she could hide behind.

So when her dear friend Bobby proposed to her,
she said,
" . . . Yes?"
even though her heart felt split.

Bobby was luminous and kind to her.
But something was missing.
Something was *wrong*.

Every day that she was married to Bobby,
she felt a little bit sadder
and a little bit more alone.

Bobby saw Lorraine was unhappy
and encouraged her to follow her heart.
So she tried—but only in her art.

Lorraine stopped writing for *Freedom* and started playwriting again. She watched plays all day. She studied scripts all night.

Lorraine knew that the country's best and biggest theaters on BROADWAY! never ran plays starring African Americans.

"So my play has to be perfect."

But every time she thought of a scene, she immediately crossed it out. Nothing felt right.
Suddenly, the tales she wanted to tell seemed small.

Lorraine worked so much that Bobby grew concerned.
"How about taking a break?"

Lorraine grumbled, but she agreed.

That night, they were out with friends when someone touched Lorraine's hand.

"You've got such a pretty voice," the young woman said.

Lorraine blushed. Her heart fluttered. She hurried away without a word.

It didn't *feel* wrong to love women, but everyone *said* it was wrong.

In New York City, it was even illegal.

So Lorraine had never explored this part of her own story.
It scared her.
She wanted to tell Bobby, but that meant admitting she was different.
It was hard enough being Black.
It was hard enough being a woman.
She promised herself these feelings would go away soon.

Desperate for a distraction, Lorraine dove back into her work.
If she couldn't be true to herself in real life,
maybe she could in her art.

This time, she asked: "What do I want to bring to the stage?"

HOME:
BRONZEVILLE.
BLACK FAMILIES.
BLACK PAIN AND
BLACK TRIUMPH.
BLACK DREAMS.

Lorraine thought of her father's early death.
A poem by Langston Hughes called "Harlem"
sprang to mind where he described
how unfulfilled dreams shrivel up
like raisins in the sun.
So that's what she would call her play.

A large family popped into her imagination.
The Youngers.
The Youngers would try to move into a white neighborhood, just like her family had.
And like her family, they would struggle.

Lorraine barricaded herself in her study and wrote, and wrote, and wrote, and wrotewrotewrote.

But the play's ending stumped her.

How could she expect her characters to be true to themselves when she wasn't?

She swallowed hard.

It was time to talk to Bobby.

"I love you, Bobby, but something is missing."
Her voice shook.

She told him that her heart beat fast around women.
She told him that she was terrified of being different.
She told him that she had to start being herself anyway.

Bobby hugged her close. "I just want you to be happy."

Lorraine was finally beginning to piece herself back together.
It was time to discover the world not as it was, but as it could be.

With new confidence, she returned to
A Raisin in the Sun.
She took the manuscript to her friend
and kindred spirit, James Baldwin.

Jimmy, as she called him, was Black, and he was a writer and he was a man who loved men.
He always told people exactly what he thought.

"Jimmy," she said. "How should my play end?"

In the play, a wealthy white man offers the Youngers a lot of money not to move to his neighborhood. He wants them to remain trapped in a dark and dingy apartment on the poor side of town.

"Should the Youngers ignore the man's offer?" she asked. "Should they accept the bribe?"

"Go the way your blood beats," Jimmy said. That meant: Follow your heart.

WHICH WAY DID HER BLOOD BEAT?

Meanwhile, investors refused to fund *A Raisin in the Sun*'s production.
They scoffed:

"A PLAY ABOUT A BLACK FAMILY?"

"WRITTEN BY A WOMAN?"

"WHO WOULD WATCH THAT?"

They wanted to twist her story into something they could sell.

Lorraine thought
and thought
and turned them all down.

"NO," SHE SAID. "THIS IS MY TRUTH."

Her story belonged to her, but it also belonged to every Black American family
who had been forced into segregation and silence.

She needed to tell it right.
Suddenly, she had an ending.
She would be true to her story—and so would the Youngers.

As Lorraine finished writing, she worried the investors were right. Maybe no one would come. Or maybe the audience would be furious that a Black woman dared to tell her story. She remembered the roar of the mob, and her stomach tightened with fear.

But she also heard Papa's warm words:
YOUR VOICE IS YOUR MOST POWERFUL WEAPON.

How many Black folks would see her play,
and be inspired to speak up?
How many would feel heard
because they finally saw themselves on stage?

But the next morning, all the newspapers buzzed.

Jimmy Baldwin poured out praise. "Never before, in the entire history of the American theater, had so much of the truth of Black people's lives been seen on the stage."

LORRAINE GLOWED.

March 11, 1959.
New York City.

"I can't believe it," Lorraine whispered.
Bobby squeezed her hand as workers changed the marquee.
Her mother and sister beamed.

A thousand people filled the audience, sharply dressed in their Broadway best.

Hollywood's biggest star, Sidney Poitier, took the stage—he was playing the leading role.

Langston Hughes bounded over just to shake Lorraine's hand.

As the theater dimmed, Lorraine's eyes fluttered closed.

When she opened them, she saw her own family on stage—Louise Hansberry, Carl Hansberry, and all of Lorraine's siblings, proud owners of their new Woodlawn home.

At the end of the play, the Youngers threw the offer back into the man's face and declared, "We are very proud people!"

They chose their dignity over money.
They said goodbye to the world as it was,
a world of segregation and sorrow,
and imagined one of equality and hope.

When the curtain swung close, the audience leaped to their feet. "Author! Author!"

Lorraine climbed onstage as the chanting exploded into applause.
Years ago, people had tried to silence Lorraine's family.
Now their voices rang out in the biggest show on Broadway.
Her father's words came back to her.
Our stories can change the world.

"You're right, Papa," she whispered.

Lorraine had spoken. And the world was listening.

Meet Lorraine's Inspirations

James Baldwin (1924–1987) was a born writer. Even when he was young, he dreamed of publishing books. He grew up in Harlem in New York City, where racism made this dream difficult, so he moved to France to have more creative freedom. During his lifetime, he composed books, plays, and essays about equality and justice. His stories highlighted the challenges and strengths of African Americans. He became close friends with Lorraine Hansberry. Baldwin was a man who loved men, and Lorraine Hansberry was a woman who loved women; they both knew what it was like to be different. Their determination to speak up helped them both become powerful writers.

Paul Robeson (1898–1976) was a man of many talents. He excelled at school. He shone on the football field. But what made Robeson truly special was his deep, powerful voice. He became a famous singer and actor who starred in plays and movies across the world. More than just an entertainer, Robeson also fought for justice: He used his fame to speak out against inequality. Robeson established *Freedom*, a magazine that gave activists a place to share their ideas. He also guided young Lorraine Hansberry in her path to becoming a playwright.

W.E.B. Du Bois (1868–1963) was an extraordinary thinker and leader. He was one of the first African Americans to earn a degree from Harvard University. Du Bois believed that knowledge was powerful, and he wrote books, articles, and speeches about how education could help make the world a fairer place. Du Bois helped start the National Association for the Advancement of Colored People (NAACP), an organization dedicated to fighting for the rights of African Americans. His writing inspired many African Americans to find their voice and follow their dreams.

Duke Ellington (1899–1974) was the master of jazz. He discovered his gift for creating music when he began playing the piano as a young boy. He eventually led a world-famous orchestra that held concerts across the world. He won many awards for his creativity and skill. Ellington wrote over a thousand songs. Many of his songs celebrated African-American culture and heritage, with lively tunes that captured the hearts of listeners everywhere. His music was like magic that made people want to dance and dream.

Freedom was started by Paul Robeson in 1950. *Freedom* was not just a magazine; it was a powerful voice for equality. It talked about important topics like civil rights and social justice. The magazine also covered global issues, showing how people in Africa and Asia were fighting for their rights. Robeson used this magazine to connect people from different parts of the world who wanted freedom and equality. Lorraine Hansberry worked with Robeson and wrote for *Freedom* while she lived in New York City.

A Note from the Author

Lorraine Hansberry was an iconic writer who refused to be silenced—her voice rang out across the world.

I was drawn to Lorraine's story because Lorraine was proud to be different. She was a female journalist when most were men. She was an African-American playwright when only white names headlined Broadway. She was a woman who loved women even though New York City declared it illegal. Yet none of these challenges stopped her. In fact, they inspired her to speak up louder.

Like Lorraine, you can speak out for what you believe in. Your words are powerful, and your voice is strong.

Although Lorraine is no longer with us, her stories continue to live in our hearts. So don't be afraid to tell your own story.

It can change the world.

Leslie

A Note from Lena Waithe

Lorraine Hansberry was an original. She was a first. She was clear about what she wanted to say. That's why her words ring so loudly. Although she wasn't on this Earth for very long, her impact is endless. Her work and spirit will live on forever.

Lorraine's legacy touched people she never even got to meet—and, as you read these words, we hope her legacy will leave an impression on you. It is up to each of us to live as truthfully and honestly as we can. If we're lucky, we'll inspire others to do the same.

Whatever your dreams are, they are important. Look after them.
You never know how far your legacy will go, and who you will inspire.

Works Cited

Perry, Imani. Looking for Lorraine: The Radiant and Radical Life of Lorraine Hansberry. *Beacon, 2019.*

Sehgal, Parul. "The Brief, Brilliant and Radical Life of Lorraine Hansberry." New York Times, *14 Apr. 2021, www.nytimes.com/2021/04/14/books/review-radical-vision-lorraine-hansberry-biography-soyica-diggs-colbert.html.*

Shields, Charles J. Lorraine Hansberry: The Life behind a Raisin in the Sun. *Holt, 2023.*

Resources

Hansberry, Lorraine. A Raisin in the Sun. *Vintage Books, 1994.*

Hansberry, Lorraine. "The Nation Needs Your Gifts." Speech to Readers Digest/United Negro College Fund creative writing contest winners, NYC, May 1, 1964. Reprinted in Negro Digest 13 (August 1964): 26–29.

Nemiroff, Robert. To Be Young, Gifted, and Black: Lorraine Hansberry in Her Own Words. *Prentice-Hall., 1969.*

Rothberg, Emma Z. "Biography: Lorraine Hansberry." National Women's History Museum, *www.womenshistory.org/education-resources/biographies/lorraine-hansberry.*

Text copyright © 2024 by Jamie McGhee · Illustrations copyright © 2024 by Loveis Wise

Zando supports the right to free expression and the value of copyright. The purpose of copyright is to encourage writers and artists to produce the creative works that enrich our culture. Thank you for buying an authorized edition of this book and for complying with copyright laws by not reproducing, scanning, uploading, or distributing this book or any part of it without permission. If you would like permission to use material from the book (other than for brief quotations embodied in reviews), please contact connect@zandoprojects.com.

Hillman Grad Books is an imprint of Zando.
zandoprojects.com

First Edition: October 2024

Design by Jessica Handelman

The publisher does not have control over and is not responsible for author or other third-party websites (or their content).

Library of Congress Control Number: 2024937457

978-1-63893-069-3 (Hardcover)
978-1-63893-136-2 (ebook)

10 9 8 7 6 5 4 3 2 1
Manufactured in China